Cai Emmons

SHORT FICTION CONTEST ANTHOLOGY

VOL 1

Cai Emmons

SHORT FICTION CONTEST ANTHOLOGY

VOL 1

ISBN: 978-1-964193-02-1

Wordcrafters in Eugene / Wordcrafters Press
434 Charnelton St., Ste 102
Eugene, OR 97401
www.wordcrafters.org
Printed in the United States of America

Table of Contents

Introduction

The Cai Emmons Short Fiction Contest honors the legacy of Cai Emmons, a celebrated author and teacher who passed away in 2023 from ALS.

Cai's writing captivated readers through imaginative stories that explored deeply human themes and complex characters. I first became a fan in April 2018 when I attended a presentation for writers in a cozy bookstore in Eugene, Oregon, where she spoke about what makes a successful writing group, on a panel with Miriam Gershow (this year's anthology contest judge) and Debra Gwartney.

Cai's warmth and humor drew me to her books, in which I found strong female protagonists navigating through a beautiful blend of the extraordinary and the everyday. This combination of magical realism, environmental and climate issues, and nuanced explorations of the human condition (especially our relationships with one another) earned her critical acclaim and devoted readers, like me.

At Wordcrafters, Cai was an adored writing instructor, offering her craft wisdom and conferences, classes, and talks.

Cai was a champion of other writers, believing we're much better off lifting each other up and supporting each other's goals.

The Cai Emmons Short Fiction Contest does just that—recognizing new voices in fiction from writers in Oregon and Washington states, who engage with the themes found in her own work, in fresh and innovative ways.

It's been my pleasure to spearhead this inaugural year of the contest and to offer you these seven short stories, each a world filled with connection, love, loss, and all the things that make us human.

Jeaux Bartlett

Associate Director

Wordcrafters in Eugene

The Winners

Grand Prize Winner

The Bechtel Protocol by Scott Colley

Female Protagonist Award

A White Cat by Elizabeth Danek

Aftermath of Loss Award

The Last Apple Tree by Justine Norton-Kertson

Honorable Mention
Gas Station Witch by Laura Grange

Magical Realism Award

The Memory Eater by Angela Ostley

Honorable Mention
Bonfire of the Insanities by Jill Betterton

Family Dynamics Award

Fragile by Erin Radniecki

Contest Judge, Miriam Gershow

Miriam Gershow (she/her) is the author of *Closer* (Regal House), *Survival Tips: Stories* (Propeller Books), and *The Local News* (Spiegel & Grau). Miriam's stories appear in *The Georgia Review*, *Gulf Coast*, and *Black Warrior Review*, among other journals.

Her flash fiction appears in anthologies from *Alan Squire Books*, *Alternating Currents*, and *Fractured Lit*, as well as many journals, including *Pithead Chapel*, *Had*, and *Variant Lit*. Her creative nonfiction is featured in *Salon* and *Craft Literary* among other journals.

She teaches writing at the University of Oregon.

A White Cat

Elizabeth Danek

South Shore ranch houses remind me of ice cream flavors. I choose the peach one on the corner.

A thick telephone directory rests on the porch. No cars, no lights, no dog. Back door jimmies easily—broken slider. Dishes on the rack bone-dry. Refrigerator hums.

Master bedroom—jewelry box. A silver necklace, cufflinks with diamond studs. Top drawer—old coins on his side. Rosary beads on hers. Mother of pearl. Slide everything into my backpack. Bottom drawer, a bayonet and grandpa's service revolver. No thanks. Kid's bedroom— Breyer horses and dolls. I rarely touch a kid's room. A dog yaps in the distance. Four minutes. This kid's room is packed with toys. I take a creamy gold horse and a white saddle with blue studs.

I grab a gem from the kitchen: a German saucepan with a stainless-steel bottom. Kid-art slathers the fridge door. Freezer check: pizza, peas, ice. No hidden diamonds. No storage above cupboards. Under five minutes—remove gloves and roll them into the bag. Three houses out of this cul-de-sac and I can be on Western Avenue.

I tuck the pan into my backpack.

The night is humid.

Next door—a vanilla ranch, pistachio trim. A Virgin Mary statue stands within a white rock garden, a wire crown of gold stars encircling her head. Pink brick border separating the Madonna from the porch. No car in the driveway. Porch light on but the rest of the house in darkness. I slip to the side door—Rita used to call it a service porch.

"Who do you service?" I asked her once and she slapped me so hard my cheek bone throbbed for a day.

A cigarette burns. I hear coughing. I gotta get out, so I slide onto the front porch. I don't see the old woman until her snappy dog growls, spins and barks, possessed. Damn.

"Seen a little white cat, ma'am?" I call through the screen as if I've just arrived. As good a line as any. The terrier's bark scratches like laryngitis. I slip my hood off.

She flinches. I startled her. Shit, I could have disappeared.

Her chair grates against the linoleum floor.

"Oh dear, don't mind Max. His esophagus is going," she says.

Before I can step away, she's at the door, trembling, blue veins splintering at her temples, boney white arms, red nose. Cataract in one eye.

"I saw a beautiful kitty two nights ago—there in that acacia tree, but today nothing."

"Thanks," I say. "Have a good evening, ma'am."

I turn to step off the porch.

"Wait a sec, hon—aren't you Millicent Costa's girl? I haven't seen you in years—Miriam, right?"

About to say no, I nod instead.

Rita always says, "Somebody's mistake may be your invitation."

"Beautiful like your mother. How's your dad? Last I heard he moved to Long Beach."

"He's good."

I slip my backpack straps to my elbows.

The old woman studies my face.

"You were, what, two years younger than my Carol. You should see her." She motions me into the house. "C'mon. C'mon."

What if Carol's inside. I can explain—your mother mistook me for—. So sorry to intrude. Lost my cat.

Creamy wainscoting runs up and down the kitchen and adjoining dining area. Somewhat unsteady, she taps the counter and a sideboard, then scuttles as if freed and grabs a picture frame from a credenza, and pumps it into my face. A pretty blonde woman, in her late-twenties, smiles, much older than me, sits with three kids on a park bench.

"Every time I see her, she's got a Big Gulp resting on her boobs. And she's expecting again." She shakes her head. "Four kids in this day and age. I don't know what they're thinking." She laughs. "Travis Sprinkle."

"She married Travis," I say.

The game's easy.

"Aah," she says as if discovering something dicey. "You liked him too—everybody did. What a smile. But that family's dying of hypertension and red dye #40, though no one listens to me. My grandkids eat cheese puffs for breakfast."

She reaches for a cigarette, the previous one down to ash.

"You mind?" I shake my head. Her lower eyelids brim red. The light outside dims. "I told the kids I quit."

"Our secret," I say. "Hey, does Carol still live in town?"

"Anaheim," she says, "though they visit a lot. Travis works the docks. Sometimes he stops by to do a project like the paneling or brings me my eyedrops."

"Maybe tonight?"

"You really want to see that boy?" she laughs.

I laugh with her.

"No, they went to Catalina for the weekend. Same as the neighbors."

No surprises. Through the backpack, I feel the Palomino front leg dig into my own.

"Put that down. Coffee?" she asks.

I agree.

"Miriam, you get the cups and saucers—there, to the right. It's decaf. I have ice cream—vanilla with syrup. How 'bout a banana?"

She hands me a large yellow one with a few brown specks, and I guess we're making splits. I take a knife from the table and cut it in half. She peels it and dunks it into an open can of chocolate syrup.

"Here, try this. Good for the heart. You got heart?" she asks and chuckles. Before I know it, I'm eating the chocolate-soaked fruit.

"Sometimes," I say to the walls, my mouth full of banana mash because she's scurrying away.

"I need the toilet, dear. You get the ice cream." Max follows her. "Millicent Costa," she mutters. I eat part of the banana, then slice the other half into one of two bowls.

I stuff her menthols into my backpack. Rita likes those. Spy a few twenties and two fives under a wire breadbasket. Leave the corner of her shopping list tucked beneath the basket with one five exposed. Pocket the rest. Lined with TV dinners on one side and a half gallon of Neapolitan ice cream on the other, the freezer resembles bookshelves.

In the middle is an ice pack and a small container with two platinum rings wrapped in a paper towel. One setting a sapphire; the other an amethyst, my birthstone. The toilet flushes. Water runs. I slide the rings into my jeans pocket, fold up the paper towel, and return the container. Outside, thunder claps.

She's humming—this little mouse. A funny little mouse, with her red drippy nose and her blurry eyes, and a family in Catalina. The dog follows her.

"I got walnuts in the pantry," she says from the hall. Now she's wearing a pastel blue duster over her stretch pants. "The kids tell me to fatten up. I'm down to nothing, I know. Georgie brings pizza and cinnamon buns. Awful combination. You remember Georgie—he's seven years younger than Carol. My oops. Good kid, but not very bright unless we talk sports. You know, food-wise, nothing appeals to me unless someone else is here. Funny how that is."

"No fun for one."

The percolator retches its last breath.

"I'll say."

She puts the ice-cream carton into the microwave, then scoops a mound into the boat dishes.

"I like it soft. No chocolate."

"Is Georgie married?" I ask. For all I know, maybe he lives in the garden shed.

"To one of the Curtis girls. Amanda, the youngest."

"Oh, of course." I nod like we're all one big happy family. "He lives near you, I take it."

"Are you kidding? With these prices. In Lakewood, off Bellflower."

"And he went to Catalina too?"

"Too expensive. I think they're home, roasting weenies." She cackles. She spoons up mostly vanilla into one dish and nibbles at a walnut. Her arms, freckled and dotted blue, swim in the duster sleeves. "Miracle Whip in the fridge door," she orders.

"You mean Cool Whip?" I ask.

She snorts between laughs. "Smarty. Cool Whip, yes! And I got those cherries. You want those—mara—mara—"

"Maraschinos."

"My husband always told me they were Dalmatian—like the dogs. He was from there. One angry son of a bitch. But you know all that." She runs the jar under warm tap water. "Thermal something."

"—Expansion," I say. She stares at me. Her eyes tear.

"You know I may be stepping out of bounds, but I think I can say it—your mother couldn't help herself. You know that, don'tcha?"

I nod. I spoon a cherry onto the whipped cream, but she motions for more. After I serve her five bright red orbs, she holds up her hand to stop me. In my bowl, giant scoops of ice cream peer through chocolate sauce moats. I dip a spoonful into the swirls, and the sugar hurts my teeth. Rita and I rarely do sweet things.

"Your mother was refined. We talked a lot. She was smart. Like you. Book smart. Life smart. She just knew stuff, but she never showed off."

She drops a cherry into her mouth, then pulls the stem away. Wish my Rita was someone's good memory.

"I been there when I was younger, and I know. Having kids snapped me out of my moods. Having kids puts other women into them." She eats a third cherry. "After your brother was born, she was not the same person. And when he died … People can only take so much."

I listen. Figure there's more.

"So, when I saw the paramedics in the garage, I knew that day. I just knew. Not like I could have prevented anything—you just don't think of all the reasons why until the moment arrives and it's too late."

The room is humid. My bra is sweaty. Max gags like an old man clearing his throat.

"It's hard to talk about," I tell her. "Every time I even think about her, I get so—I—"

"Then take some medication, honey. Nowadays, they have drugs for everything—not like when my dad was young or your mom. And you need to talk things out. It doesn't have to be with a head doctor. I tried that after Matt died, but this psychologist gal made me so nervous, I'd come home from her office and pour me a highball."

"I'm fine," I tell her. "It was a long time ago."

"At least ten years."

"Longer."

"But losing a parent so young, that affects you." Ice cream melts into the sauce. I press the cold spoon against my cheek. A clap of thunder in the distance rolls with the clouds.

"I do miss her."

"Of course you miss her. She was beautiful. Her stories. At times, I hear her voice. Talking to Millie felt like you were the only two in the room. That lovely hair. And you have her eyes. We talked a lot about you kids. She loved you—never doubt that."

Good old Millicent. Heavy air. My throat tightens.

"The kids say I talk too much. Like the time I asked Mrs. Radovan when her baby was due, and she wasn't pregnant. Carol almost killed me." She wants to pour coffee, arms trembling. "Do you mind, Miriam?"

I fill her cup.

"Remember Mrs. Radovan, the seventh-grade teacher? Math and Science. Don't think she taught you kids much but she was a smart dresser for her size." She laughs and waves her hand over her belly. "Carol said it was hormones. She taught you about overactive and underactive thyroid." She laughs again and coughs past a spasm and waves for water, which I pour.

"Thanks," she says. "She's gone."

My face must show that I'm lost. My neck starts to cool.

"Mrs. Radovan. She died last Saturday. Colon cancer. Funeral's on Friday. Think I'll do the rosary and skip the mass. Catholics overdo everything, don't you think?"

I'll check the obituaries. Empty house.

"Her husband living?'

"God no. Joe died ages ago. And Joe, Jr. was killed right after Carol graduated, remember? What a mess that was."

"Who gets the house?"

"A niece in Riverside, I heard. Won't even be here for the funeral."

"God, yeah, awful." I scrape my bowl clean. She eats the last cherry, but the ice cream is an ivory puddle. I wash my bowl and wipe every surface I've touched with a dish towel, the table, cupboard handles, refrigerator and freezer doors, under the basket, the cooler. I take her glass in a napkin and rub it clean, faking the discovery of a stain.

"Oh, that's just my lipstick, Miriam. Makes me feel human." Rita would have no patience for this mouse. "I'd always see your mother after mass. In those days, we went to church."

In the distance, the fog horns bellow, like when I'm in a deep sleep and the blankets are warm and I smell the harbor from my window. Rita's in the kitchen, and she wants to know if I have any money. I ignore her. I hear her on the bus. I hear her at the pawn shop. Now that she's blind she talks more. "Just listen to me goddammit," she starts. Yesterday she says, "Don't say a word. You can spoil rotting food."

"Sometimes memory is just enough," the old woman says. She sips her coffee. She spoons her ice-cream slop into her cup. "Would you like some scrambled eggs? Cream of Wheat?"

She takes another cigarette. The sugar brings me down.

"No, thanks. I'd like to get back before the rain."

Max growls as I rise.

The old woman blinks a few times.

"I thought your father sold the house."

At the pantry, she rummages through cans and packages. "Take these, Miriam. I haven't even asked—are you married?" She hands me a box of cream-filled wafers. "I thought I had some nuts."

"No. Just a cat."

"Ah, yeah, a white cat. Where do you live, dear?"

"With a friend. In—Gardena."

She smiles.

"A pretty name for an ugly place. Sweetheart, leave me your phone number. Next time Carol visits, maybe you two can get together or meet here."

She rummages for a pen and paper from the sideboard.

"If your father moved to Long Beach and you live in Gardena, what are you doing looking for a cat in the old neighborhood?"

"Long story," I say.

She wants to help me. I slip my arms into the backpack straps before her white, boney fingers touch it.

"You always loved animals, I remember."

She reaches for me.

"Every kind."

"Sometimes it's good just to see where we came from." She pats my back. "Millie," she says absently.

"Miriam." I correct her.

"Leave your number, dear."

"Why don't you give me yours," I say.

She writes her number quickly, and I take the paper with both hands, then let her hug me—her chest and back so thin, so easy to break. I slip the number into my pocket.

"Sometimes when I didn't have a hope left in the world, it was your mother who listened," the old woman says and pats my arms. "You're so much like her."

I feel like slapping her narrow, wrinkled face. I hate being compared to Rita, who sucks the air out of a room. Maybe this one can, too, with her stupid son, pregnant Carol, and the fat science teacher. This little mouse! Rita once threw my Breyer horse at me and missed, but the front legs hit the coffee table, which I called the coffin table because it looked like one. A horse leg snapped off and Rita threw the whole thing away. "No gimp toys." I took it out of the trash, glued the pieces together, and braced it between two books. Days later, she found it and laughed, breaking off all the legs in four easy snaps.

Mice eat their young.

I glance at the stupid cuckoo clock. Fifty-two minutes. I push the screen door open with my elbow and wipe the outside handle with my sleeve.

"Say hi to Carol and Frank."

"Georgie." She corrects me.

Lavender and rosemary blend with the dense air. I wave from the driveway and watch as her thin arms against a pink wall, white as lightning, wave back. Goodbye, mouse.

In the distance, a foghorn groans. The sky roils. Storm ahead.

With my bandana, I take out the Palomino, wipe it down, and leave the horse and the pretty blue saddle on the neighbors' porch. Then I head toward the bus stop on 25th and Western.

I pass a newsstand in front of the supermarket and deposit the coins, recalling the kids at school always featured in the paper for sports or Kiwanis Club or the spring musical and, when they passed by the newsstand on 13th and Gaffey, and one kid dropped in a quarter, they took all the papers— fifteen, twenty or more—and divided them up, hunting for their pictures and the stories. I could never do that. It's called an honor box for a reason.

My chest hurts.

The Radovan obituary is in the paper and online. The photo maybe forty years old. A pretty woman. I find the home address on my phone.

Rita will be on the porch, tapping her cane, complaining about how I left her alone for so long. I'll let her touch the German pan. Let her wear the rings until we hawk them.

Near the corner, I pass more homes with ice-cream paint—mint green and pink.

The mouse could teach her something. Millie Costa did.

I release a gasp, a sob. The pain subsides.

The neighborhood is quiet.

Quiet as a cat.

Elizabeth Danek (she/her) was born in San Pedro, California, and earned a Master's in Humanities from Cal State Dominguez Hills. Her stories have been published in *The Writer's Workshop Review*, *Mid-American Review*, the *Los Angeles Times*, and *Flash Nonfiction Food*, as well as performed for Liars' League PDX. She has taught high school English and adult education in Los Angeles, California; Munich, Germany; and Portland, Oregon. She is currently working on a novella and a collection of stories. She lives in Milwaukie, Oregon.

The Last Apple Tree

Justine Norton-Kertson

The orchard isn't really an orchard anymore. It's one tree—a crooked, wind-scoured, fruitless apple tree clinging to the last patch of good soil on a hillside.

Down below, Fall Creak wanders past. All around, the Willamette Valley lies hushed, stitched with the long scars of what once was: cracked irrigation ditches, a rusted tractor half-swallowed by the golden grass of a long-abandoned seed farm, the faint outlines of rows that no longer hold anything worth naming.

Mara leans against the handle of her spade, catching her breath. The earth smells of rain—thin, hard-won rain that came at dawn and left almost as quickly. It's been years since the downpours came the way they used to. These days, rain passes over the hills like a stranger unwilling to stay. Still, the tree has managed another bloom. Its blossoms tremble in the afternoon wind, pale and fragile against the blue-washed sky.

She kneels and begins clearing the weeds around the roots, fingers sinking into the damp soil. The bark under her palm is warm, rough, and familiar. She knows every knot, every scar. Elena's grafting knife left a crescent here—a tiny, clean wound where life took hold again after the blight. Mara presses her hand there in the same way one might touch a gravestone.

Wind threads through the blossoms, lifting the scent of apple and loam. It's the only scent that has ever meant home to her.

By evening, the light has thinned to amber lying soft on the hill. Mara climbs the narrow path from the cabin with a mason jar of honey wine swinging lightly from her hand. She made it herself, the way Elena taught her: wildflower honey, well water, and patience. It tastes sharp and sweet, like memory.

She sits at the base of the tree, knees folded beneath her skirt, and raises the jar.

"Here's to you, my love," she says. "Another year. Still standing."

She pours a trickle of wine into the dirt and takes a sip. It burns just enough to remind her she's alive. The tree's branches rustle faintly—not the sharp chatter of wind, but something slower, more deliberate. She frowns, glances up. The air is still. Yet the blossoms seem to be moving, each petal stirring like a small hand brushing sleep from its eyes.

"Don't play tricks on me now," she whispers. But her voice softens as she says it, because part of her wants it to be a trick. Part of her still listens.

When the ritual is done, she sets the empty jar against the trunk. Her gaze traces the fungal ring climbing the bark—chalky and white, higher now than it was last spring. She's tried everything she knows: compost tea, charcoal wash, pruning. It all just slows the inevitable. The tree is dying. Not this week, maybe not this year. But soon enough.

The research center has written again—three letters she's tucked unopened into a drawer.

"A rare genetic survivor," the last envelope said through the window before she turned it over. "An important specimen." She doesn't need to read the rest. They want clippings, tissue, cells. To her, this isn't a specimen. It's Elena. It's the shape of a precious life they built together.

She rests her brow against the bark, breathing in the sharp green of the leaves. For a heartbeat, the world goes still. Then—just at the edge of hearing—a tremor moves through the orchard. A listening silence. As if the hill itself has taken a breath.

Mara steps back slowly, unsure whether it's the tree or her own heart that has answered.

Morning comes gray and wet. A thin fog clings to the lower valley like an animal that doesn't know where else to go. Mara pulls on her boots, fills the tin watering can, and starts her slow circle around the orchard's ghostly perimeter.

There are no other trees left, but she still walks the lines as if they were there—forty-seven steps east, thirty-two south, a soft turn by the row where the cherries once bloomed. Her hands remember what her eyes no longer see.

She kneels to pluck a weed curling around a forgotten post, and the scent of crushed grass opens a door in her memory. Elena, laughing with her hair tied up in a kerchief, planting the first saplings in a spring that smelled exactly like this—green and sweet and shy. Mara can still feel the slickness of the earth between their fingers and toes, the way Elena hummed songs without words as she tamped down the soil around each root.

Another step, another trigger.

The rusted irrigation spigot catches the light just so, and suddenly it's the summer everything burned. Heat shimmers over the fields. Trees cracking like porcelain under flame. Apples blackening on the branch before they fall. Elena's voice calling her name through the smoke. The orchard dying one tree at a time.

And then, the night they saved this one—the last apple tree. The blight crawling like fire through the rows. The two of them on their knees beneath the smallest tree, hands sticky with sap and soil, grafting a branch from one that hadn't yet sickened.

"We can save this one," Elena said. "One's enough."

The tree lived.

Elena didn't.

Mara stops beneath its boughs now and runs her thumb over the crescent scar where the graft took. Elena's last words echo through her—not spoken in the hospital, but here, beneath these branches, when the air still smelled like apples.

"Keep it alive if you can. And if you can't—let it go."

The fog lifts by afternoon, leaving the world sharp and empty. Mara's boots leave deep prints in the soft ground.

The first whisper comes at night. Soft sound threads through the dark, finer than wind. Mara steps outside and wraps a quilt around her shoulders as the cold slaps her cheeks awake. The tree stands silver under the moon, its blossoms catching the pale light like wet shells in the sand.

There—again. A whisper. Not words at first, but cadence. Elena's cadence. The way she used to breathe between sentences.

Mara stands barefoot in the mud, breath caught in her chest. The sound brushes past her ear like a gentle fingertip.

"Wait," the whisper says.

The night holds its breath with her. She presses a hand to her sternum as if to steady something fragile inside her. The wind doesn't pick up. The blossoms don't move. But something in the air feels like it's listening. Present.

For the first time in years, she isn't alone on the hill.

The next morning, a truck rattles up the dirt road—a sound Mara hasn't heard in a long time. She wipes her hands on her skirt as a woman climbs out, young and sunburned, wearing work boots too new for the mud.

"I'm sorry to just show up," the woman says. "I'm Nina. We've been tracking heirloom survivors. I've been hoping to find this tree."

Nina gestures to the apple tree as though it were an artifact. Mara feels the first hard tightening of her jaw.

"It's not a thing," Mara snaps.

Nina pauses, then explains how few genetic holdouts have survived the blight, how this particular rootstock might still hold dormant resistances, how they could graft it and grow entire new groves if it takes. She opens a neat little black case—grafting knives, sterilized tape, specimen bags.

"I can take just a cutting," Nina offers. "You wouldn't have to—"

"No." Mara's voice comes out soft but certain. The world blurs at the edges as her eyes swell with quiet tears. She steps between the girl and the tree. "It's not a specimen. It's my wife."

Something flickers in Nina's face—discomfort, maybe, or pity—but she doesn't press. She closes the case and leaves her card in the mailbox anyway.

"If you change your mind," she says.

Her boots crunch down the gravel road, and the sound of the rattling truck fades into the distance.

Two days later, the bees come.

Mara almost doesn't notice at first—the air is so rarely alive with sound anymore. But a low, golden hum grows at the edges of the orchard. A handful of bees, feral and battered, weave through the blossoms like small survivors. Their wings look like scraps of old glass. She stands very still and watches them work, dipping into flowers that shouldn't have bloomed this year at all.

She remembers the hives Elena built—wooden boxes painted sunflower yellow. In the mornings, they'd sit with their coffee and listen to the hive singing, the orchard alive with flight and pollination—with life. Elena swore the bees spoke to the trees. Mara used to laugh and pretended not to believe her.

The hum grows thicker, rounder, wrapping around the apple tree like a spell. For the first time in a long time, the place feels connected to the world beyond the hill—a fragile thread, but real.

Mara closes her eyes. She can almost hear Elena laughing again.

The second whisper comes on a night clear enough to see the faint smear of stars above the foggy valley.

Mara wakes to it again, softer than a sigh at first. She walks barefoot down the path, the air sharp against her skin. The tree gleams in the moonlight—its blossoms brighter than they should be, their scent sharp and sweet, like the orchard at its height.

"You don't have to hold on for me."

The whisper flitters by on a momentary breeze that doesn't touch Mara's hair. The sound is so like Elena's voice that Mara nearly drops the lantern. It isn't a perfect reproduction—no ghost would be—but the inflection is hers. Elena, speaking with the same tempo she did when she was tired but sure. When she meant something.

The petals above shimmer even though the air has stilled. Mara lifts her hand, and a single blossom drifts down, landing against her palm as softly as breath. She feels the weight of remembering like a stone in her chest. Years spent trying to keep the orchard alive when the world beyond it had already moved on. Years spent clinging to this tree as if it were a heart she could keep beating by sheer will alone. She doesn't know if she's ready to let go. She doesn't know if she ever will be.

But what she does now know is that she's not alone in this grief. Something—Elena, memory, perhaps even the land itself—has been speaking back.

The moon climbs higher, silvering the branches. Mara stands beneath the blossoms, the lantern's flame guttering in the breeze. After a moment, she whispers into the night, "I hear you."

Petals rustle faintly in reply.

The storm tears into the valley like a hand unbuttoning the sky. Already heavy air thickens with the sweet-sour scent of blossoms and ripening soil. Wind whips across the valley in a single long exhale, rattling the rusted fences and sending the first brittle branch snapping like a matchstick. Clouds boil over the ridgeline. Mara's body feels the warning before she can name it: the storm isn't passing. It's coming straight for the hill.

She barely has time to throw on her coat before the first gust slams the cabin door against its frame. Rain sheets down the hillside in slanted gray lines, pooling in the irrigation scars and turning old grass seed farms into new swamplands. The last apple tree thrashes in the gale like a creature trying to root itself against a tide that won't yield.

Then she hears it—the crack of light—deep, wet, like a bone breaking too close to the ear. The tree splits down the center, lightning-white along the graft scar. A shudder moves through the ground, through her, as though something inside the earth itself just gave way.

Mara stumbles out into the storm barefoot, mud squishing through her toes and sucking at her ankles. Wind claws at her hair as she falls to her knees at the base of the trunk. The tree leans like an old, tired giant. Rain pours into the split, soaking the heartwood. Blossoms whip into the air like frantic birds, vanishing into the torrential night. A car engine grinds on the road below. Headlights flare weakly through the rain.

Nina.

She fights her way up the hill, soaked and panting, her black case clutched against her chest.

"Mara!" she shouts, voice distant against the wind. "I can still take a graft—we can save it!"

Mara doesn't look up. Her palms press into the split trunk. Beneath the soaked bark, through the churn of the storm, something speaks. Another whisper, not from the wind this time—not Elena in the air, but Elena in the earth. A vibration beneath her hands, low and warm and utterly familiar.

Mara, the roots say.

She closes her eyes. She can see Elena's hands on the grafting knife. Elena's hair in the sun. The orchard when it still held its breath like a living being. This tree isn't Elena—not exactly—but it's the last place in the world where her voice still lives.

And now, even that is breaking.

Nina shouts something else—practical words, urgent ones—but they're distant. The only sound that matters is the pulse beneath Mara's palms. She's finally ready to listen, truly listen. The whispers weren't begging her to hold on. They were asking her to let go.

Mara stands. Her hands shake, not from fear but from the terrible weight of understanding. She takes Nina's grafting knife. The young woman doesn't stop her.

She makes a clean cut, just below the split—a single living branch, still slick with sap. It's enough for one sapling. Not an orchard. Not a monument. Just a future.

She lays the knife down in the mud.

"I'll let you go," she whispers, to the roots, to Elena, to herself. The storm answers with a gust so strong it bends the trunk toward the ground. The tree groans once—a long, aching sound. Then, it gives way.

Wood splinters.

Tears fall.

Branches crash.

Hearts pound.

Soft wet petals whirl upward like prayers set loose into the night.

Mara doesn't run. She stands in the rain with the graft pressed against her chest, watching as the last apple tree falls.

The storm's gone by morning, but it leaves the hill hollow. The tree lies split and charred, roots yawning toward the pale sky. A silence settles over the land—not the comfortable kind, but the stunned hush that follows something too big to name.

Mara spends the day gathering what remains. She saws the trunk into pieces small enough to lift, her hands steady and deliberate. When the sun drops low, she drags them to the old orchard's edge and builds a pyre from wood and memory. The smoke rises straight into a sky still bruised from the storm.

She burns it all. Every branch, every leaf, every blossom that clung on through the night. When the flames die, she gathers the ashes in a tin bucket and carries them to the base of the hill where the orchard meets the meandering waters of Fall Creek. There, in the spongy, wet earth where the orchard's first tree once stood, she digs a shallow hole. She pours the ash in gently, like laying a loved one down to rest.

The bees return at dusk. A thin, fragile ring of them hovers above the soot-stained ground. Their wings catch the last light like stained glass, and their low hum fills the space where wind used to whisper. It sounds like a vigil.

For the first time in years, the hill is utterly still.

For the first time in years, so is Mara.

Weeks pass. Spring leans into early summer, and the valley greens again in shy, thin patches. The earth doesn't heal quickly anymore, but it hasn't forgotten how.

Mara hikes down the hill toward the edge of the creek, carrying the graft wrapped in burlap and string. It's rooted now—a sapling no taller than her hip, thin as a wrist, a tremble of green leaves at its tip.

She doesn't bring tools—just her hands. And in the same spot where she buried the last apple tree's ashes, she digs a hole with her fingers. Dark earth curls beneath her nails as she places the sapling. She presses the soil gently around its base until it stands on its own, fragile and defiant.

She doesn't name it. She doesn't claim it.

The river wind moves through its leaves, and the scent drifts upward—soft and sweet, like a recollection too faint to hurt.

A child's voice startles her.

"Why are you planting a dead tree?"

It's the neighbor's little girl, mud streaking her boots, hair tied back in a frayed ribbon. She's standing a few feet away, hands behind her back, watching Mara like she's peering into a secret.

Mara wipes the dirt from her palms and straightens slowly.

"Because," she says, "one day, it might want to live again."

The girl frowns at that, the way children do when they meet a language bigger than their years. But she nods solemnly, as if she understands something anyway.

On the walk back to the hill, the air is warm and soft. The river hums at her back. Mara feels the rhythm of her own breath moving easily in her chest for the first time in years.

And then she hears it—not from the wind this time, not from the blossoms or the soil.

A laugh. Elena's laugh. Light and brief and real, stitched into her breath like it's always been there, waiting.

Mara doesn't turn back.

The hill is quiet now, the old orchard laid to rest. But down below, by the river's edge, a young sapling shivers in the breeze, its new leaves catching sunlight for the first time.

Justine Norton-Kertson (they/them) writes fiction, creates games, and is editor-in-chief of *Solarpunk Magazine*. Their short fiction and poetry have appeared in *Utopia Science Fiction Magazine*, *Reckoning Magazine*, *Jupiter Review*, and others. Their nonfiction book, *Utopian Witch: Solarpunk Magick to Fight Climate Change and Save The World*, was released in July 2024 from Microcosm Publishing, and their debut horror novella, *Gutterspace*, is out in October 2026 from Stars and Sabers Publishing. Justine lives in rural Oregon.

The Memory Eater

Angela Ostley

My grandmother spoke of the Memory Eater like medicine. A salve to smooth scars that puckered skin. A purging tonic to exorcise demons. Give him your grief and nothing more. A cleansing—for the small price of remembering.

She spoke also of warning. What might happen if you give too much. How pain becomes lesson. There is a balance, she cautioned. How, if we do not let our suffering teach us, we become only a different form of stuck.

I was not scared of his taking, or of a loss of my own choosing. I thought only of release. I knew the legends. Knew the way from her stories.

He lived at the edge of all cities like an outcast—an open invitation waiting for anyone willing to walk down his path.

When I visited the Memory Eater, I meant only to erase the hurts that haunted me. To loosen the chains that choked my lungs and, just maybe, breathe a little easier. I sought out his cabin, hidden back in dark woods. I was eager. Desperate for a lightness I hoped he could grant.

When I knocked, knuckles on stained oak, the door swung wide in darkness like a throat set to swallow me whole. He invited me in, his table bare and eyes already full, and I did not yet know that I was the meal.

He had candles spread, reminding me of church. Should I say grace, thank something in the ether for the loss I sought to be rid of? Confess my sorrow like sins?

He beckoned as he sat, long fingers placing a cloth napkin across his lap, and I took the empty chair beside him. He was so tall he hunched, and still his head nearly scraped the chandelier. It, too, was full of candles, lit and languid in their melting.

I took him in. He was fearsome, though I felt only his warmth. The promise he offered. His eyes seemed black in the low light. Hungry and pulling like the vacuum of the night sky, though no light from any stars pierced that dark.

"You seem thin," I said to break the silence, a small laugh escaping my lips. "Are we living such easy lives these days that there are no horrors left to feed on?"

I tried to cover my unease with a joke in a way that had become habit. Drowning the hurt in humor. He looked through it like glass.

"You have memories for me." It was not a question. "It is why you are here."

His fingernails clicked on the wood of the table like seconds ticking away. Long and yellowed, like maybe he was sick. He saw the question in my eyes.

"The memories do get weaker over time," he told me. "They don't sustain me. The flavors run thin, and the taste eludes me." The way he said the word "eludes," drawn out like oil over the tongue, made me shiver.

He asked for my pain first. His eyes burned with hunger. His long fingers curled against the table. Eager, though trying not to appear that way.

"I did bring something," I offered. I had lived, long and well. Most of my memories, I had to admit, were comfortable. They fit like old clothes. They made me smile when I thought of them. But some of them ached. Some of them festered. I had carried that pain long enough. I would give it to him gladly.

I did not have to dig deep to conjure the memories I chose. All laced with loss. Edged in pain, if not pure agony through and through. Red-tinged and sharp—the ones that still cut. I thought of a war veteran removing shrapnel from an old wound. I wondered briefly if, when it was gone, it would still ache when it rained. If there would be some lingering echo of the explosion that put it there. Let him cut it out. I had no need for war trophies.

I gave him first the day my father died. An old woman I had never met, her voice on the telephone explaining what happened. The image she painted of him, alone in some house on the coast I couldn't picture in my mind. I had never visited him there. I gave him that guilt as well.

I gave him his death, too many pills in his guts, a half-eaten sandwich on his chest. I gave him her apologies, the way my knees went out from under me, the way my entire world tipped and spilled its contents like some violent earthquake. The way the sound went shallow. The way my chest burned. The way my stomach turned. The way my mind wouldn't.

He licked his fingers as I described it to him. Vulgar, almost, the way he languished over each word. Sucking, gorging. Gasping, as if I did not utter them fast enough to satisfy.

Gone was the echo of the way I had cried. Gone also was the way I had lifted myself from the floor afterward. I felt a space there like a hollow, feeling the shape of it though I could not remember what it had held.

"More," he said behind glistening teeth.

The loss I had come to surrender was gone. I could leave, perhaps even should.

His hungry eyes pulled—a gentle nod as he watched me consider. What could it hurt, to set down a bit more of my suffering, when it was plain that he wanted it. Needed it. Was asking for it with the licking of lips. I had more to offer.

I gave him my heartbreaks, one by one. The silly, childish hurts like the sandy-haired boy who had told me I wasn't that pretty or the stolen kiss on another girl's lips. The running mascara and the tied-up phone lines. He ate them like candies, rolling them around on his tongue before swallowing them down. A hum in his throat, eyes closed in pure ecstasy.

I gave him also the grown-up devastations. The broken bottles. The hurled insults and fists. The brake lights that bled a rage-filled face red in my rearview. The woman at the airport, alone in a strange city, wondering how her life led her there. He slurped my suffering like a savory stew poured down his throat in violent gulps. Consumed it with rapture.

As he ate, I felt lighter. The pain and sorrow of my life—he drained from me like nectar. Relished it even, as I watched it dribble down his chin. His long, fleshy tongue sweeping out to catch every drop that escaped his lips.

I began to give him other memories. Not quite so sharp and deeply wounding as the pains I had offered so far, but scars that might bleed if I dug hard enough at them. I gave the red ripping of my body when I gave birth to my son. The moment of fear before the cry. The hospital room my grandmother had taken her last breath in, the final beep of life support coming to a stop. I gave him a car crash on rain-slicked streets—the blue and red pulses of light. The hand on the glass at the county jail, cold black phone to my ear.

I even gave him the time I fell out of the catalpa tree. I was nine and near fearless. Taller than the whole world as I climbed, gripping and pulling up toward sky. When the branch snapped beneath me, I fell like a stone. My spine smacked solid ground, wind rushing from my lungs. I remembered the fear when I couldn't pull in breath. Fear that I would suffocate in my own body. Fear that I would never breathe again. Die right there below the cracked branches and raining leaves.

He ate, and I gave. Euphoria swirled in as the anguish ran from me like silt down a drain. It spread through my veins, muffled bees in my blood. I soared—the lift, the release in my bones like I had never known, making me dizzy with its lightness. Why had I not done this sooner? How easy to hand these broken pieces of me over. How freeing. Now it was I who wanted more.

I chose then to part with the mundane. The giving had become easy, and the Memory Eater ate it all with abandon. I gave him my job. The hours, days, years spent at a desk. The meaningless work, the drivel. The college assignments, the essays, and tests. All that knowledge I wasn't using anyway. Let him have it.

I gave him a leisurely hike down an alpine trail in Autumn where I had twisted my ankle on a tangled root. Leaves swirling in reds and golds. A grimace and a twinge. A book I had read and thought horribly written. A book I had read and never finished. My taxes—neatly filed. A bee sting on my wrist. I gave him the glitter of a too-cold lake I had plunged my feet into. The chill against my skin. My summer laugh.

I did not notice that the memories I served up like delicacies on a platter were no longer colored with hurt. The way I carved myself like an apple, good flesh going with rotten. I did not notice the flesh purpling around my eyes. The insulation of fat and muscle earned over years thinning out. The bones at my wrists arching high like mountain peaks. My shirt hanging loose from hollowed collarbones.

The Memory Eater reached with sticky fingers. He gnawed on the bones of my life, sucked the marrow from inside. Picked it from his teeth.

When I had given him every memory I was willing to part with, I asked him to stop. I saw my face reflected in his shining eyes, glossy with repletion. I did not recognize the woman who stared back. I had let him take so much of me. Eaten away to bones. Feasted upon.

That sorrow had shaped the lines above my brow. That pain formed the arc of my hips, wrenched wide to bring forth one life, and then another. All definition had gone—all the details and the fine lines that composed me smudged away. Like a crude outline of a person, I was fading into nothing. All the things that had made me, he had swallowed, and what remained? Only my joy, my most precious moments. I realized too late that it may not be enough to walk out of there with. To remain corporeal and whole.

"Aren't you full?" I asked.

His belly distended, cheeks round, fingers drenched in all he had taken. His movements were slower, less frenzied than before. He licked his lips, tasting.

"Almost," he purred. "But not quite. Not before the very best part."

He smiled wide, his pointed teeth slick and dripping with the remnants of my life. My belly felt hollow. Concave and shriveled inside my weakening bones, carved out like a holiday carcass. Nothing but scraps to be picked clean.

"Now is the dessert." He rubbed his hands together, eyes gleaming. "All that sweetness, those golden, honey-dipped delicacies you've been saving." A wicked desire in those dark eyes. "Just a taste."

I didn't want to offer those. I tried to cling to them, to hold them beyond the reach of his hunger. The smell of my baby's head, just washed, downy wisps of hair as he slept. My husband's hand gripping my waist as we spun together under twinkle lights in the dark. The full moon over a lake—not a single sound but the chorus of crickets. My mother's hands. The names of my friends, spoken so many times they wore their shape into my mouth.

He took, and he took. Plucked each bite from me like an expensive truffle. I watched as he placed them gently between his lips. As he wrapped his tongue around my happiness and chewed. I felt the bile rise in my own throat as his moved with each swallow, taking them forever from me.

I began to feel hunger, then. A deep and drowning want, though I didn't know for what. I felt delirious, unsteady as I tried to rise and found the body beneath me all jutting bones and skin stretched taut over it like translucent canvas. Hideous blue veins webbed across my hands and my feet. My jaw ached, and my teeth clacked. My fingers looked too long, too thin as I reached for sustenance and found only his empty table.

The Memory Eater was gone. I was alone— what was left of me.

Was this my home? I found I didn't know what home should mean, what it was for me. It seemed someone should be there beside me, but I had no thought of who. I belonged to no one, and no one belonged to me. There was only emptiness. Nothing to remember, nothing to hold onto.

There was nothing there to chew on. Nothing to satisfy the need my clenched teeth felt. The need to press down into something substantial. Something with meat.

I needed to eat. To feed. The thought spread through my blood, a fiery need.

A knocking reverberated through the cabin, quiet and dark. A fist on solid oak, the pounding echoing through the halls.

I passed the table where candles had been lit. Two chairs pulled out, inviting. I stalked to the door and gripped the handle with my wasted hands. Pulled it open onto the dark.

There stood a woman. Young, though her shoulders were curled as if she were old. As though the weight of something heavy pulled them down.

Tears streaked down her face. Fingers clutched the collar of her coat together at her throat. She cried softly, making small sounds as I beckoned her inside. It was warm, I told her. Safe from whatever troubled her out there.

I smelled her as she passed through the doorway and nearly fell to the floor. Savory, spiced. So full of flavor. So full. My mouth watered. My stomach clenched. I led her inside to the dining room, where an artful display of candles was lit. Fresh and tall, just starting to melt.

"Come in," I coaxed. "Sit down at my table." I knew it was my table, though not exactly how. I lived there. She had come seeking me. Let us see what she had brought.

"Please," she cried. "I have lost everything that matters to me. Everything but the images that keep me awake long into the night." She choked on her sob, then continued.

She spoke to me of a small child, with hair as bright gold as the rising sun, with a laugh that rang clear as spring water. She spoke of the tangled bedclothes, the sweat, the stillness, the cold. The heartbeat she never found. Her screams—ripping hair, hands tearing at her eyes, pleading. The silence, hers and another's.

"Please," she said again in a whisper. "Take it from me."

I felt the pull in my throat, the scrape of my teeth against tongue at the taste of her words. I wanted it to fill me and fill me and fill me until I burst.

When the woman placed her grief in my hands, I opened my mouth and began to eat.

Angela Ostley (she/her) is a poet and fiction writer whose work blends tenderness and teeth, exploring grief, moral tension, and feminist defiance. Her poems have appeared in several literary journals, and her short story "Shifting Stone" was published by Forest & Fawn. She lives in Vancouver, Washington, with her husband, two children, and two dogs, where she drafts stories and scribbles lines in between the chaos of everyday life, grounded in the stubborn belief that words can both wound and mend.

Bonfire of the Insanities

Jill Betterton

When my sister was fourteen, she swallowed a snake. It was small, and at first, it didn't take up much room in her stomach. She still had room for dinner, but not dessert. When our dad grilled steak or our mother baked bread, the snake stirred in her stomach and made her feel sick.

Over time, the snake grew bigger, taking up more and more space. It hurled pancakes and bacon out of her stomach and writhed around in protest if she drank too much milk. It stretched its ugly head out of her mouth, screaming for crickets and live mice, none of which my sister could abide. She'd collapse on her bed, exhausted and wracked with guilt for refusing to give it what it wanted.

"I just can't," she sobbed. "It's just too gross."

She'd placate it with grapes, lettuce leaves, and a few carrots throughout the day. It would settle down in her stomach, grumbling and squirming in the shrunken space.

She grew thinner and thinner. Her arms and legs became spindly, and her abdomen was so skinny that you could see the snake roaming around just below her ribs. The skin on her face stretched over her cheekbones and turned sallow. She hissed and slithered around the house, flicking her tongue at anyone who came close.

Our parents sent her to a snake charmer who tried to coax the snake out of her stomach. The snake curled up in a ball and seethed while my sister sat through the whole affair with clenched teeth. When the snake charmer's flute failed, he tried incense, cookies on a plate, a pair of jeans my sister had coveted for the last two months. The snake dug in its fangs, hanging onto the edge of her stomach. Banging snare drums, air horns, and even a sedating elixir were tried next. Nothing, it seemed, could make the snake leave.

My sister grew angry and yelled at our parents.

"I just don't understand," cried my mother. "What in the world made you swallow the snake?"

My sister glared at her. The snake flicked its tongue between my sister's teeth as she hissed at my mother and stomped her feet. It seemed as if she wanted the snake to stay.

So our parents sent her away to a large brick building three states away. The brochure claimed it had snake charmers, a magician with potions to help her gain strength, and poison for the snake.

"It's a fortress!" she hissed. "A prison," she spat through gritted teeth as my parents led her to the car.

I stared out the window as they drove off with my best friend, my heroine, sobbing in the back seat.

She stayed there for six months, locked up like Rapunzel, her hair falling out in clumps rather than growing long. Eventually, the snake gave up and withered into a ball the size of a small egg. She kept it weak with pills and eventually ingested food that the snake had previously hated. It was too weak to protest.

When she came home six months later, her pinched face had grown round, and her arms and legs had flesh that covered her bones. Our parents were giddy. They cooked her favorite foods, took her to the movies, and bought her new clothes. She looked over her shoulder as she walked out the door with them for yet another treat, leaving me to wallow in front of the TV.

"Sorry kiddo. It's what they want."

Her eyes clouded over, and I caught a glimpse of something wiggling under her shirt.

One evening, she came into my room and sat on my bed. She looked at me with her soft brown eyes and laid her hand on my foot.

"Listen my compatriot, my partner in crime. I need you to do something for me. I'm going to a bonfire and need you to come along."

I pulled my foot away and folded my arms across my chest.

"We haven't had any adventures together in over a year, and you certainly didn't include me when you decided to swallow a snake."

Her eyes grew moist, and she wrapped a strand of hair around her fingers.

"I know," she said, hanging her head. "But that's why I'm going to the bonfire tonight—to get rid of this snake for good. And I need you to come along."

"A bonfire. What's that have to do with anything?"

"Me and some of the other kids from the fortress, I mean clinic. We've all been treated now, but well, here we are, not quite done. We're sick of our insanities. We're going to burn them in a giant fire tonight."

I scooted back on the bed and tucked my feet under me.

"You're not insane," I said vehemently.

"Well, I think swallowing a snake is the definition of insanity. I'm not ashamed." She tossed her hair behind her. "Anyway, I need you there, to help me get the snake out and throw it on the fire. Get rid of it for good."

I gasped and pulled my knees up to my chest.

"You're burning animals!! Oh no. Count me out. Ask Mom or Dad."

My sister reached out and put her hands on my knees.

"I can't. They don't know the snake is still there. You are the only one."

She cocked her head to one side and offered me a weak smile. Her hands trembled slightly on my knees.

I sighed.

"Fine. Let me get my shoes."

We took the bus to the edge of town and then walked along the road until we came to a patch of trees. Clouds drifted across the half-moon in the gray sky and crickets chirped in the tall grass on the other side of the road.

"Here," she said and led me along a narrow path.

She turned on a flashlight and guided us to a clearing where a huge bonfire blazed.

Half a dozen teenagers were standing near the fire. One had a bird on her head that kept pulling out strands of hair. She wrenched it off and held it tightly around the neck. A chubby, dark-haired kid flicked at spiders that crawled up his arms. They spun a web around his head and arms so thick he struggled to see. Other kids dug in their ears and pulled out long worms or wrangled cats that scratched at their skin.

Behind them stood siblings or parents. A few had a gaggle of friends.

One skinny kid stood alone, no parents or siblings around. His hair was greasy and hung in lank strands. His arms were covered with red streaks, and a capuchin monkey clung to his back. He reached up to swat it off, but it batted away his hand.

My sister grabbed my hand and pulled me toward the group.

"Are you ready?" she asked the other kids, her voice echoing above the crackling fire.

The teens nodded and murmured replies.

My sister held up her hand towards me and said in a hushed voice, "You need to stay back, but close enough to catch me if I fall."

My hands were shaking, and my legs felt weak. Before I had a chance to voice my objections, the girl with the bird screamed, "Get off of me. Stay away from my God-damned hair!"

She twirled the bird over her head by its neck and flung it into the fire. People gasped and someone screamed. It might have been me. But the bird didn't screech or go up in flames. It evaporated into a puff of grey smoke that drifted off into the woods.

One by one, kids flung their spiders, fistfuls of leeches, worms, and feral cats. The fire crackled and blazed, and tiny puffs of colored smoke disappeared into the sky.

My sister opened her mouth and leaned toward the fire, but nothing came out.

Her belly rolled and bulged, and the snake slithered up her throat, latched onto her mouth with its gnarly fangs, and snapped her mouth shut. She panted and flailed and then opened her mouth and reached in with her hand and grabbed the snake. She flung it into the fire and roared.

A yellow and black cloud of smoke hovered over her head, and she collapsed to the ground. I rushed to her, took her in my arms. As she lay on the ground sobbing, her smoke evaporated until just a tiny puff remained.

The bonfire died down. Tearful, spent teens walked back into the woods, held upright by relatives and friends. Except for the kid with the monkey who'd come alone. He crept back into the woods, the monkey still clinging to his back and pinching his neck.

I took my sister's hand and pulled her to her feet. We walked through the woods, the smell of damp soil and bonfire smoke hanging in the air. The pale, half-moon illuminated the path just enough so we could stay on the trail.

When we got to the road, my sister turned and looked at me. She pulled my beanie off my head.

"Should have thrown this in the fire," she said as she spun it on her finger. "Anyone who's still wearing a Spiderman hat at thirteen has to be insane."

I jumped for the hat as she held it over my head, and we laughed and laughed, and the tiny puff of yellow and black smoke drifted farther and farther away.

Jill Betterton (she/her) is a writer of short stories, although she's currently working on a novel. She's a member of Wordos in Eugene, Oregon.

Fragile

Erin Radniecki

Joanna willed the water to pull her paddleboard forward, aiding her escape as she slipped away from the dock and toward the tall grass.

She imagined her title of parent slipping away, too: lifeguard, sunscreen applicator, food provider, complaint sounding board. All day she had waited for this quiet time before dusk when she could sneak away, her one responsibility playing with cousins under the watchful, if indulgent, gaze of grandparents.

Joanna sighed. Indulgent, loving, freighted. She imagined that weight, too, slipping away as she stroked, putting space between her and her family.

Just as she had done in her youth, Joanna avoided the deep water, choosing instead to paddle along the edge of a mass of reeds and cattails nearer the shoreline. She wasn't afraid of the deeper water; she just preferred to stay close to shore where life was more easily observed.

As a child in her father's boat, she had learned that the middle of the lake may supply the largest fish, but the edges provided the most activity. Compressed between sand and sky, lake life by the millions ate and were eaten, hunted and mated.

She snaked along a winding path of gaps in the tall lake plants. The stiff, tubular grasses rubbed against the inflated polyethylene she sat on, like a herd of tiny trumpeting elephants, announcing her arrival as she pushed through.

Joanna grinned at the thought of a line of small pachyderms standing at attention, their trunks raised. Keri-Lynn would like that image, she decided. Well, she corrected herself, would have liked. Her eight-year-old daughter had loved Joanna's fanciful descriptions—until recently.

Many things had changed recently, Joanna had noticed. Just like her mom, Keri-Lynn had grown up with an insatiable passion for animals and the environment. Even in preschool, she boldly saved worms stranded on drying sidewalks and transported housebound spiders outside to safety.

But lately—suddenly—it seemed Keri-Lynn couldn't care less.

Joanna always knew her daughter's interests might change, but now that it had happened, it hurt more than she had expected. Perhaps because it was an identity they had always shared, or because it was the first concrete sign of her child putting distance in their relationship. The first of many, Joanna thought.

Or was it something more? Joanna had a nagging fear that she had failed to instill her love of nature deeply enough that it could survive her child's youth. Had Joanna done enough to make sure Keri-Lynn could be surrounded by modern temptations and still stay grounded in knowing her place in the natural world?

With this worry in mind, she had invited Keri-Lynn to come out on the lake that evening.

"There's an extra board, and we won't go far," she had said, trying to coax without pushing. "I usually see some pretty neat things. Turtles, and stuff." She had shrugged, as if she wasn't desperate for an affirmative response.

"No thanks, Mom. Laine and I are going to paint our nails tonight. She just got some gel polish that sparkles and glows in the dark."

So here Joanna was, alone on the water.

"Never mind," she said to the lake. "I can still enjoy myself."

It always surprised her how quickly she took to paddleboarding each year. Sure, she felt some muscles more acutely—the little stabilizers in her knees, ankles, the tops of her feet—reminding her it had been a year. But in no time, she was comfortable again, following her yoga instructor's direction to ground down through all four corners of her feet more urgently here than she ever did on the mat.

She loved her time on the paddleboard; it was one of her favorite parts of visiting her family each summer. Of course, she could paddleboard at home in Washington, but it just wasn't the same as being on her lake. Maybe it was the Midwest humidity, or the smooth glassiness of a smaller lake. Perhaps the waters of the Pacific Northwest were a bit too wild, influenced by their cousin, the ocean, and fed by their neighbors, the mountains.

Whatever it was, she cherished her time on the water here and greedily took as much as she could get. A chance to be yet one more creature, keenly observing as she was observed. She loved the solitude, the way she was alone yet in the center of so much. A guest, uninvited, but attempting not to impose.

Was it so different from her status in her parents' house, she wondered. Invited, of course, but avoiding imposition all the same. Every visit trying to fit in, to tone down her herness.

She had always been different, the dreamer of the family. The one with ideas, the one who got quizzical looks while her siblings received praise. Her family never seemed to understand her, though she knew they tried. She just cared so deeply about so many things, so many creatures. Her imagination was always feeding her stories about the wildlife around her, how they were getting along, how humans were hurting them.

It had been a relief in college to find others who thought like her, who cared about the environment as passionately as she did. She had embraced everything she learned with a zealousness akin to religiosity.

During every break, Joanna came home and regaled her family with all she had learned. There might have been some critiquing and judging, too. In her exuberance, Joanna failed, or chose not, to read the room, until her mom put a stop to it.

"You love nature so much, but you make me hate it, you know that? I can't look out my window and enjoy seeing my own garden without your voice in my head pointing out how it's all wrong."

"Mom, I'm not saying—," Joanna started to defend herself.

"No. You let me finish. Instead of appreciating the flowers, all I hear is you complaining about non-native plants and fertilizers and pesticides. Well, I'm done with it. I will not have you coming into my house and lecturing me."

Joanna rested the tip of her paddle on the board and rolled her neck, as if she could release the discomfort of the memory like stiffness from a muscle. With the hindsight of middle age, she knew her mother was right. Joanna had been too pushy, too judgmental, and just so damned constant. A mosquito droning her message of sustainability into everyone's head. Well-meaning, but irritating just the same.

That moment marked a turning point in their family. Joanna had always been different, but after that day, she realized something fundamental had changed. Something had broken, and she had caused it. Now every visit, every phone call, and interaction came with strings attached. An unspoken agreement that certain topics weren't to be discussed.

For her part, Joanna had tried to avoid anything that could be interpreted as a critique of her parents' way of life. But children introduce complications to any dynamic, and as soon as Joanna and Paul announced they were expecting, the packages began showing up. And kept showing up. A regular drip of clutter, all of it pink, sparkling, noisemaking, and battery powered.

"You don't understand how hard it is for us, being so far away from her," Joanna's mother would say. "We're just trying to keep things fair between all the grandkids."

Joanna let the board glide for a moment, stilling her paddle and taking a deep breath. Fresh air in, bad energy out. If she wasn't careful, she'd spend the entire outing stewing about her family instead of paying attention to the lake she loved.

Joanna directed her board into a space surrounded by cattails, an aquatic sitting room just large enough for a single board and rider to maneuver. The resident red-winged blackbirds protested, unappreciative of guests, especially humans.

Standing in the little reed room seemed impolite, so she sat down and extended her legs onto her board, leaning back on her elbows.

What a curious space, she thought. Except for the small entrance, she was completely hidden. Maybe she would move in with the blackbirds. She could be like an aunt to all the baby birds she knew were in nests woven within the cattails.

She smiled at herself. Another story that would have captured Keri-Lynn's attention while also reinforcing Joanna as the family's dreamer. How had she ended up so different from her parents and siblings? It was as if she had inherited all of the family's imagination. Is that what made her so attentive to nature? She could imagine the experience of the animals around her, could empathize with them?

Joanna listened to the chatter of birds around her as they gossiped about neighbors, children, spouses. She predicted similar gossip about her occurring back on shore.

She sighed, imagining the discussion between her parents, her siblings, and their spouses. Why she lived so far away. Why she got so worked up about plastic. Why Keri-Lynn was an only child.

But no, those subjects weren't really what her family would be talking about this time. They were old topics, hashed and rehashed for years, like flavorless gum gnawed out of habit.

Her family had long decided that she and Paul had stopped at one child because of sustainability concerns. They had never considered that there was another reason, and Joanna didn't bother to correct them. Somehow, it was easier having them believe she was self-righteous rather than infertile.

She looked down to find a pair of citron damselflies on the nose of the board, shamelessly engaged in their heart-shaped mating formation. Within hours, the female would have laid her eggs within the plants of the lake and moved on. How simple for them, Joanna thought, no longer jealous of creatures with procreative abilities.

Joanna's arms itched to move, so she stood up and pushed her way out into the open. The birds escorted her as she left, following with a song of good riddance and don't return, which, despite their efforts, she found pleasantly melodic.

Joanna pulled hard against the water until her arms ached. She focused on the discomfort, her shoulders on fire, sweat trickling down her back beneath her life jacket.

No, the latest gossip would be around Paul's absence from the family vacation this year. It had been a surprise to Joanna when he informed her, just as she was about to buy tickets, that he wouldn't be joining them.

"I can't stomach the carbon," he had said when she asked why. "You and Keri-Lynn should go. It's you two they really want to see. Plus," he added cheerfully, "we can save the money."

"Save the money," she said aloud to the lake, striking the paddle against the water. As if money was her concern, not the loss of his company. Not the loss of his reassuring presence as she carefully treaded the dangerous waters of natal family togetherness. Not what everyone would think.

She and Keri-Lynn had been in her parents' house not two hours before her daughter came to her, eyes wide and full of tears, to ask if Joanna and Paul were getting divorced. Joanna knew exactly where the idea had come from. Damn it, Jenny, she had thought to herself as she tried to reassure Keri-Lynn. Her brother's wife never wasted any time sowing seeds of trouble wherever she could. And even if Jenny wasn't callous enough to say something directly to Keri-Lynn, her son Dylan certainly was.

Joanna shook the memory from her head and willed her attention to her surroundings. She was surprised, as always, by the brilliance of the water around and beneath the board, the details clear like cut glass. The angle of the late-day sun illuminated the underwater plants in vibrant greens, browns, and yellows. She saw a turtle beneath the water and smiled, allowing its auspicious presence to lift her spirits. Startled by her silent appearance above, its wide paddle-feet clawed the water, pulling it down to safety away from her threatening presence.

"That's right," Joanna said. "Stay clear of angry moms."

She paused in mid-stroke. She was angry, often. Just last week, she had noticed it was becoming her response to any disturbance, as though she had been poked and pushed so many times her skin had become thin and fragile. The realization had surprised her. When had anger become her default emotion?

Joanna sat down on her board to think. What did she use to feel, before she was angry all the time? Surely the anger had replaced some other emotion. She tried to think back. Before anger, there was exhaustion, and before exhaustion, there was, what?

"Trying," she said aloud to the lake. Trying to balance everything. Trying to provide life lessons to her daughter. Trying to arrange a suitably sustainable lifestyle for her husband, which of course clashed with the lifestyle of a modern parent, not that he noticed. Trying to placate her family while still holding on to her values.

Trying. She turned the word over in her mind, like a stone meant for skipping. It felt right. Trying to make everyone happy.

How many times recently had she realized she was talking to herself? *It's fine. It's fine. I'm fine.* An agitated mantra repeated as she moved through her day. But even though she tried, it wasn't always fine.

And now her Keri-Lynn, her fierce little naturalist willing to go to battle for the creatures around her, no longer seemed to care. She was more interested in dolls, dress up, makeup—all the things that never appealed to Joanna. It felt like more than child separating from parent. It felt like a betrayal, and it was exhausting to try so hard and be abandoned. No wonder anger showed up in its wake.

But what other choice did Joanna have? Cave and let her daughter descend into a consumption mindset? Align with her Luddite husband and force a do-without lifestyle on the family? Let the gifts from her parents come at will and ignore the garbage can overflowing with packaging? How was she ever going to teach Keri-Lynn what was important in life if she couldn't stop the battle in her own brain?

A cool breeze reminded Joanna it was getting dark. Her eyes had adjusted to the setting sun as she had let her mind wander in circles. Now the sun was dipping, but she was no closer to a resolution.

She knelt on the board, close to the water, to use her core muscles as she directed the board toward the dock. She entered the tall grasses again, slower on the return trip, wanting to delay as long as possible.

Her lower height brought her attention to the detritus of the plants. Young dragonfly nymphs and old shed skin both clung to reeds. Ragged cotton from last year's cattails next to this year's, just green and forming. Dense plants, still loud with birdsong, holding new eggs and old nests. It was as if the plants were keepers of the lake's memories, holding onto the past alongside the present.

What would her past and present look like, held in the long fingers of lake grass? A youth of certainty and idealism, the lack of responsibilities making every decision appear easy. A present of exhaustion, endless choices, and battles to fight or abandon. A future unknown.

It all just seemed so fragile. Keri-Lynn's childhood, her marriage, her relationship with her family, the planet. Where should she dig in, and what should she let slide?

As she emerged from the reeds, she could hear the commotion of young voices getting louder. Joanna sighed. Better resume her role as parent and attempt to tame the wild things hyped up on sugar and marketing.

There was enough light left that she could see Keri-Lynn, dressed in a sparkly princess dress, running with her cousins, shrieking with laughter. Wait, was it laughter?

"Dylan, you stop that right now."

Joanna recognized the edge in that voice, moved beyond roughhousing to actual anger. Dylan was the oldest of the cousins, and his banter could border on bullying. Joanna paddled faster in case she needed to referee.

"Dylan!" Keri-Lynn screamed this time.

Joanna leapt from the paddleboard, dragging it just out of the water, and bounded onto the grass, ready to save her child. She was so intent on intervening that she was stopped short by what she saw.

There was her daughter, pink sparkles and all, threatening her cousin with a marshmallow roasting stick. Her hair was wild, and even in the almost darkness, Joanna could tell she was both irate and near tears.

"Do you know how many species of fireflies are going extinct, and you're just killing them for fun? How would you like it if I squished you and spread your blood on my arms? Open the jar, Dylan. Do it now!"

"Hey, Dylan, better knock it off or Keri-Lynn's gonna take out one of your eyes." Joanna's brother was suddenly by her side, calling off his progeny.

"You got a live one there," he said to Joanna, grinning.

"I didn't know she was paying attention," Joanna said, more to herself than to him.

"Oh, come on now, it's been pretty obvious that apple was going to land close to the tree. Why do you think we try to spoil her? It's the only way the rest of us stand a chance. She'd be hell to live with if she turned out just like you."

He leaned over, bumping her shoulder gently with his as he headed up the hill to the house.

"Mom!" Keri-Lynn bounded up, the previous battle already forgotten. "Look at my nails! They look like fireflies!"

"They're beautiful, Keri-Lynn," Joanna smiled. "Maybe you could paint mine too?"

Erin Radniecki (she/her) is a fiction writer and Author Accelerator-certified book coach based in the Willamette Valley. She explores themes of nature and community in both her personal writing and in guest posts featured by Jane Friedman. When Erin isn't reading or writing, you can find her gardening for pollinators in her backyard.

Gas Station Witch

Laura Grange

Susan stared down at her husband Charlie's lime green camp sandals, sitting neatly at the edge of the hot spring pool. Steam rose from the water, a slightly eggy smell that she still hadn't gotten used to.

It was his idea for them to become volunteer camp hosts at Trinity Hot Springs. They were about halfway through their post-retirement round-the-country road trip when they reached the little campground in eastern Oregon. It was beautiful and well-treed, and he loved soaking in the hot springs—three small pools tiered into a hillside. "I'm tired of driving," he said. "Won't it be nice to stay someplace awhile?"

Despite Charlie's waiting sandals, all three hot spring pools were empty. Susan scanned the rocky area surrounding the hot springs, then the tree line. It was early, the rest of the campground still asleep, and the quiet was unnerving. She tried to focus on the water spilling from the top pool to the middle to the last; to the sound of water gently flowing down, down, down.

When the Silver Alert went out to every phone in the state, she was mildly amused. She imagined how outraged her husband would be when he saw it. How indignant. Serves him right, she thought. Disappearing on me like this.

She was less amused when, after a week of searching with no sign of him, they brought in two cadaver dogs. She watched as they passed her camper, holding Charlie's little white dog, Norman, tightly to her chest. A thick heaviness, like wet cement, filled her up—solidifying quickly and so cold.

Norman lost it for the both of them, his tiny furry body shook with outrage, his yapping bark loud and agitated.

Charlie had found the dog a few weeks into their road trip in Norman, Oklahoma, when they stopped at a Whataburger for lunch.

The dog was in the parking lot, his little head shoved into a greasy paper takeout bag, curly tail wagging as he gobbled up cold fries. His long hair was dirty and matted to the skin; his nails so long they curled inward. Charlie snatched up the dog and spent hours in the back of their camper washing, combing, and cutting until he uncovered a skinny, white-haired Maltese mutt. She suggested they take him to a nearby shelter, but was outvoted when her husband insisted Norman get a vote, and he raised a paw for "stay with us forever."

So, when they left Norman, Oklahoma, Norman, Dog went with them.

The cadaver dogs didn't find Charlie, but they did find the decaying body of a hiker reported missing two months earlier and the skeleton of a young girl, the skull smashed to pieces.

Eventually, the police officially gave up looking for Charlie and moved his case to some filing cabinet drawer they never opened again. No leads, no evidence, so sign of Charlie. She was told she needed to let go, move on.

She wouldn't give up on Charlie. Couldn't move on. She extended her stay as camp host indefinitely. Every day, she imagined new potential scenarios: chopping firewood and looking up to see him strolling towards her, his green camp sandals back on his feet where they belonged, as if he'd only been gone a few minutes. Or her phone would ring, and she would hear his warm, laughing voice on the other end, "Susie! You'll never believe it, but somehow I ended up in Alaska!"

At night, she slept on the right side of the bed as she had for forty years, clutching Norman to her aching chest. He nuzzled his little head into her neck, and sometimes she dampened his fur with tears and snot, and sometimes she didn't. She slept with her back to the vast chill of Charlie's side of the bed. The emptiness where the outline of his body should be.

A year passed. She couldn't leave the campground even if she wanted to. Charlie had never taught her how to drive the gigantic RV. All she knew how to do was signal from behind the monstrous vehicle: yes, the brake lights are working; yes, the turn signals are working.

Without Charlie to maintain things, the camper began to break down. The propane ran out, the exhaust fan stopped working, and the decorative trim was peeling off the walls. Susan sat on the bed, looking around her at everything that needed fixing or cleaning or refilling. Each chore a wave crashing over her, again and again, pulling her under.

The campfire crackled and spat while Susan sat in her rusting camp chair, absentmindedly petting Norman while he snored softly in her lap.

Across the road from her campsite, voices echoed into the night. She looked over at them warily, two young couples sitting around a campfire, drinking. A blonde, shaggy-haired man with a stupid-looking mustache was standing while the others sat, gesticulating with his arms, his voice amplified with alcohol.

"Okay, so, a few months ago, Jen and I were driving along in our old truck and were super low on gas, right? So we stop at this kind of old, crappy-looking gas station we came to in the middle of absolute-fucking-nowhere."

His girlfriend, Jen, apparently, sat quietly in the chair next to him, peeling the label off a beer. Brown hair spilled in front of her sharply angled face, large doe eyes turned downward.

"The place was really old, like from the 1920s or something. It only had one pump and a shitty little shack for a store. We weren't sure it was even still working, but we had to try, right? So we pulled up to the pump and waited for the attendant, but no one came. So Jen gets out to go see if anyone is inside the shack—"

At this, the woman in the other couple broke in.

"You didn't go in with her? She could have been murdered!"

The blonde man's face flushed briefly, and he looked down at the ground, then at his girlfriend.

"Well, I thought—I just thought she was using the bathroom or something. Anyway, she's in there for a while, and then she comes out. She gets back into the car and just sits there for a minute, not saying anything. And I'm like, 'Well? Can we get gas here or what?' and she just shrugs and—Jen, you wanna tell them what happened inside the shack?"

Jen looked at the couple with tired eyes. This was clearly a routine he did, a well-rehearsed play, and now it was her line. She sighed and took over the story.

"Well, I go inside, and it is basically what you'd imagine. Old gas station store, a few shelves with some dusty bags of chips and candy bars. No cooler or anything. There's an old woman behind the counter reading a newspaper, so I go up to her and ask if we can get gas. She looks up at me and smiles. She says, 'Is that what you're really looking for? Gas?' Well, I was a little confused; it was a gas station."

"What she was looking for!" the blonde man crowed, smacking his forehead theatrically. "Gas!"

Jen paused, her gaze sliding down to the crackling campfire in front of her.

"Yeah, so I repeated, yes, I was looking for gas. The woman gave me a strange look, like she was disappointed or something. She shrugged and said, 'Okay.' Then sort of waved me out of the store."

Susan noticed the other woman giving her husband the same *let's get out of here* glance she used to give Charlie at just about every social function he dragged her to. Like Charlie, the husband didn't seem to notice.

"So Jen gets back in the car, and when I turn it on, it had a full tank of gas! We'd been runnin' on fumes and all of a sudden out of nowhere we had a full tank. At first, we thought the gauge must be broken, but we drove one mile, then two, then five, then twenty, and the car kept goin'."

He looked back at Jen, who nodded but didn't look up from the campfire.

"We never filled that truck up again—we've been driving ever since on that one tank of magic gas."

Susan felt herself leaning too far forward in her lightweight camp chair. She corrected herself before she and Norman fell over into their own campfire.

"So, you got what you asked for? Gas?" the woman in the other couple asked.

Jen shrugged.

"I guess."

"Couldn't have asked for a billion dollars!" the man exclaimed, shaking his head in exaggerated disbelief.

Susan waited for the trick, the con, the ask, but none came. The man just opened his cooler, held a beer up in offering to the other couple. They both shook their heads no and pulled themselves, not without effort, from the camp chairs they'd been sinking into.

"Well, gettin' late," the man said. "Early morning tomorrow."

"Oh, sure, okay," the blonde man answered, deflated and disappointed he was losing his audience.

The other couple left, and Susan watched the blonde man and Jen for a few moments before making up her mind. She stood, dragging Norman along by his leash as he made a low grumble-growl sound he often made when he was unhappy with a situation.

"He-llo there!" she said as she approached, bending her face into an attempt at a smile. "I'm Susan, the camp host."

She pointed at her camper across the road, where a small wood sign swung with the words "Camp Host" carved into it. "I couldn't help but overhear your story, and was wondering… Um… Where did you see this gas station?" She tried to smile again.

"Well, that's the thing," the blonde man answered. "We actually came across it not too far from here, it was off the 224, near Ripplebrook." He pointed in what seemed like a random direction. "But—"

"We went back," Jen inserted softly, her gaze on Norman, who, already bored, had lain down at Susan's feet and was nibbling at one of his paws. "We went back to where the gas station had been, but it was gone."

"Gone?" Susan asked, eyebrows raised.

"Gone! Poof!" the man agreed, snapping open a PBR and taking a deep swig. "Never saw it again."

Susan eyed the battered truck a few feet away and nodded towards it.

"Is that the same truck?"

The man nodded and burped.

"Same truck."

Susan took a small step backwards, suddenly struck with the suspicion that they might try to sell her their magical truck since the other couple hadn't taken the bait. The "Jack and the Beanstalk" story came to mind. Well, she was old but she still had her wits and wasn't interested in magic beans or magic trucks.

"Well, better get to bed myself," she said as she turned to leave. "Let me know if you need any more firewood, $5 for a bundle."

"We won't, leaving tomorrow morning," the man said before sinking back down into his camp chair. Susan nodded and gently pulled Norman's leash, who begrudgingly lifted his tiny body from the ground and followed her back across the road to her camper.

When she woke up the next morning, the couple—and their magic truck—were gone. She stood staring out the window at the now-empty campsite, the prior night's story digging into her mind.

She thought about the gas station as she cleaned the campground bathrooms. She thought about the gas station as she cooked pasta on the small stove in the RV. She thought about the gas station when she stared down into the steaming hot spring pools, her early morning ritual.

She took to walking Norman around the campground, talking to campers, slipping in questions about a mysterious gas station that granted wishes. All she got were confused and concerned looks.

She was walking Norman past a family of four—the father staring at his phone as the mother yelled at her two kids to *stop climbing on that* and *stop hitting your brother* and *what did you just put in your mouth,* when Norman spotted something in the brush. With a quick twist of his head, he slipped out of his collar and bolted away, his little white body disappearing into the growing dark of the trees. Susan stared at the limp leash in her hand, Norman's collar dangling uselessly at the end.

The forest surrounding the campground was too dense for her to follow the dog except for the few paths cut in. She half-ran around the perimeter of the forest toward the nearest trail in, screaming in a tight, breaking voice she didn't recognize, "Norman!"

Her nails dug into the nylon of the leash as she searched, the panic she had tried to stomp down, to control, bubbled up higher and higher inside her until it felt like it was about to burst from her mouth, her eyes.

In the next campsite she passed, a woman was on her knees, struggling to get her campfire going. She lit a match, tossed it into the pit, and blew—a gray puff of ashes burst up into the air, but nothing caught. Her young son sat in a camp chair nearby, short legs swinging. Susan slowed and squinted at the boy—at the little white dog in his lap.

She hadn't seen a dog with them when they'd checked in, but that didn't mean they didn't have one. She approached the site slowly, squinting at the dog, trying to make sure it was Norman before she interrupted them with accusations of stealing her husband's dog. Her dog.

"Norman!" she whisper-hissed. The dog's little head popped up, swiveling until his gaze landed on her. His little curly tail started wagging.

She rushed over to the woman, sweaty and huffing, short of breath.

"Excuse me, hi," she said as nicely as she could manage. "I believe you have my dog."

The woman looked up from the campfire, her face and hands streaked gray with ash, a look of frustrated rage across her face. She turned and looked at her son, the dog in his lap, then back to Susan. Her face relaxed, and she stood, wiping her hands on her jeans.

"Oh, is he yours? He wandered over, and Ryan's just been petting him. He loves animals. Ryan, give the lady her dog."

Ryan pouted a little but scooped Norman into his arms and slid awkwardly out of the camp chair. He held the dog carefully to his chest as he walked over to Susan. He offered Norman to her, and she took him, sliding his collar back over his head and tightening it so it wouldn't come off again. She squeezed her eyes shut, forcing the tears back, and pressed a quick kiss to the top of the dog's head.

The woman was back on her knees, blowing more ash into the air.

"Do you need some help?" Susan asked, pulling herself together. "I'm kind of a campfire expert."

The woman looked up at her again and smiled slightly.

"Yeah, that'd be really nice, thank you." She slowly stood up. "I've never actually done this before, but he insisted we go camping after his friend told him about some trip he'd gone on, I don't know. Here we are."

She waved her arms at the campsite as if she'd done a magic trick—ta-da!

Susan smiled and nodded, handing the leash to the boy.

"Why don't you hold onto him for me while I help your mom, yeah?"

The boy smiled wide and took the leash from her.

She picked up the cheap ax they had brought and began chipping thin slices from a log and arranged the kindling carefully inside the metal fire pit ring. Susan glanced up at the woman and asked her what she'd been asking everyone she met lately.

"Have you ever heard of a magic gas station?" Her hands didn't stop moving as she built up the firewood into a perfect teepee shape. She kept her eyes on the mother as she lit a match and saw what she had been so desperate to see since she first heard the gas station story.

Recognition. She lowered the lit match to the kindling.

As the fire caught and grew, the woman told her a story similar to the one she had heard before. Coming across a gas station in the middle of nowhere, meeting an old woman in the shack.

"When she asked me what I was looking for, I said 'a cure.'" She looked over at her son, who had his arms wrapped around Norman in a tight hug.

The little dog looked over the kid's arm at them as if he were listening to the story, too.

The woman's eyes became glossy in the firelight. She lowered her voice.

"He had leukemia—the doctors had said he wouldn't make it to his sixth birthday. He'll be eight this year. I don't even know why I said that to her. I guess finding a cure was all I thought about back then."

Susan hesitated before asking.

"So the cancer…?"

"Gone." She shrugged. "I've never been religious, I don't believe in much, to be honest. But I sure believe in that gas station witch."

Susan walked down to the hot springs one last time and stared down at the spot her husband's sandals had been.

"Everything is going to be okay, Charlie," she whispered.

"I just need to go get some gas."

Laura Grange (she/her) explores layered female characters, complex relationships, and evolving connections with the natural world in her stories. She has served as an editor for several literary journals and currently works for a nonfiction book publisher. She lives in Seattle, Washington, with her husband and dogs.

The Bechtel Protocol

Scott Colley

Sarah awakened slowly from the dream. She liked to log dreams in the notebook by her bed, but her mother was yelling second warning, so she staggered to the bathroom and into the shower before the water could warm.

She ran across the frost-crusted grass while the sun, cold, peeked over the hills. The school bus was leaving, but stopped as she approached.

After wiping cold droplets from the window, Sarah again thought of her dream. The sun, fully up now, gained warmth and color. The dream was fragmenting, but the nuance of it stayed. In it, she was encased in a sleeping chamber aboard a starship. She had just awakened, her eyelids too heavy to open. Her school lessons were completed while she slept, and she knew about the stars, the starship, farming, engineering, and much more. She had been sleeping for so long and there was still far to go.

The dream slipped away. Sarah watched the sun move higher and felt it warming her skin.

Alicia awakened slowly, her eyelids heavy. The cryosleep chamber hissed away its pressure.

"Alicia, get up. Activity time."

Alicia ran the treadmill, did a yoga routine, and a variety of other exercises.

"Fanny?" A younger Alicia had been allowed to name the ship's computer, and Fanny had seemed like a funny name for the AI.

"Yes, Alicia?"

"I dreamt I was on Earth."

"You dream that often."

"Do I?"

Hard to remember other dreams. She woke every six days for exercise, every ten days for comprehension testing, and every…

"Fanny, how long have we been underway?"

"134.641 years, Alicia."

"How long to go?"

"104.234 years."

Alicia pulled the resistance bands.

"The sun was coming over some hills, bright but cold. Frozen grass made a strange noise as I ran over it. I got in a yellow transit vehicle with white plumes of exhaust. The sun moved higher and warmed as we moved. I felt it on my face, Fanny."

"An interesting dream, Alicia. Very Earth-sounding. Time for your chamber."

The pod top hissed closed. Its air mix immediately made her sleepy.

"Fanny?"

"Yes, Alicia?"

"Will I ever feel the sun on my face?" She fell asleep without hearing the answer.

Over the years, Sarah continued to dream of Alicia in her starship. The dreams were troubling because of their consistency and the feeling of being in someone else's mind. Sarah was always Sarah in her other dreams; scared Sarah or laughing Sarah or flying Sarah, but always Sarah. In the Alicia dreams, Sarah felt both herself and Alicia. It frustrated her to be Alicia yet not as smart as Alicia.

The knowledge Alicia possessed was always just beyond Sarah's comprehension.

In her sophomore year of high school, Sarah won the Ogeturk Award for her simplification of the Henri Paradox. The award historically went to a graduate student's dissertation, but her math teacher had sent her work in.

Sarah was embarrassed by the attention, partly because she felt that she could solve the Paradox and the simplification seemed insignificant. But most of her embarrassment was due to being head over heels in love with Carson Jenkins, a senior and demigod at school. Sarah wanted him to notice her, but being known as the local math genius was not what she had in mind.

The day of the award ceremony, Sarah decided to walk home after school instead of taking the bus as usual. It was a warm spring day with large cumulus clouds floating above, the pollution and UV indexes safe. A perfect day to walk. The math award bothered her. Her parents were thrilled. Sarah wasn't sure she even liked math. It was just there, always running in the background. She knew it was Alicia. Sarah sat on the grass hill in Alabaster Park, halfway home. Her thoughts flittered back and forth between Alicia and Carson, both enigmas. She watched the clouds pass, island-sized fluffs of moisture. She could see Carson's face in one of the clouds.

Retention testing days always left Alicia with a headache. Studies showed that subconscious education was superior for retention and best for categorizing and organization. She thought that probably no one had done a study on how hard a person had to work to pull that subconscious data up into the conscious mind.

"Fanny, why did people on Earth see things in clouds that weren't there?"

"Do you mean the shapes of animals or things of that nature?"

Alicia liked it when Fanny hesitated a moment before answering. She pretended that Fanny was looking desperately through billions of bits of information to find an answer. Technically, Alicia knew Fanny had all the data for everything instantaneously, and any hesitation was just incomplete data in her query, but she loved the idea that Fanny could be flustered.

"Sure—animals, castles, boys' faces."

"A lot of the cloud shapes will have similar shapes to familiar objects, such as elephants or dragons. Often, the cloud shapes are amorphous, and the viewer is more likely to see things they have been thinking about, like gods or boys' faces. Are you interested in this subject?"

"Not really."

Alicia had stopped telling Fanny about her Sarah dreams. Not that she didn't trust Fanny, but the Sarah dreams felt personal and not to be shared.

"Just curious."

"Hmm, okay."

As always, Fanny knew Sarah better than herself and probably knew where the question originated.

"Your test scores from today are low in 'Politics and Climate Crisis of the 21st Century.' We'll run you through that history again in your next sleep cycle."

"Ugh, all right. I think I have it—but I don't understand it."

Alicia could not grasp how issues on Earth could have progressed so predictably and tragically, yet been ignored and exacerbated beyond humanity's ability to fix them.

"I mean, how could the people be so stupid? It doesn't make sense."

"You are correct, Alicia. It was not rational, but human history shows time and again that people are not always rational. We'll talk again after your next cycle."

Sarah's dissertation at Princeton University on a new theory of propulsion necessary for interstellar travel split the world's astrophysics community in half, one group jumping on the opportunities for new math and science, the other calling it flawed logic. Time would prove Sarah's theories correct, but that didn't make her immediate post-doc life any easier. Her department had insisted that the dissertation be named the Bechtel Protocol, though she had thought something without her name would be better.

NASA and other space agencies contacted her about consultations. Sarah wasn't sure what she wanted to do.

Before her dissertation, she had received a few offers from universities and nearly convinced herself that a life of quiet academia was what she wanted. Private companies offered her unlimited budgets for research and previously unimaginable salaries. She was particularly wary of these.

"Alicia, wake up. We need you on the bridge."

Fanny's voice was no different than ever, but Alicia felt the urgency. For her scheduled awakenings, her sleep chamber brought her up slowly, warming her to a natural temperature over hours. Now she was shivering and sluggish. Of course, she had never been called to the bridge, either.

"What's going on, Fanny?" Her teeth were chattering, and her body didn't want to respond to her commands.

"Sorry for bringing you up so quickly, Alicia, but the ship is not responding correctly to its programming."

Alicia forced herself out of her pod and pulled on her workout suit. The suit's temperature settings immediately increased to counter her low body temperature. She left her room, stiff-legged and groggy.

"Give me more information, Fanny."

The bridge was a twenty-minute fast walk away.

"We have been slowing for the last 300 days as we've approached the target solar system. In the last six hours, we have veered three degrees off the Bechtel Protocol parameters. Bridge engineers think there is another force pulling the ship off course. They have not been able to correct the drift."

"Hmm, not my field of expertise…"

"Apparently, even our experts are outside of their expertise."

The bridge was fully staffed and noisy. This was the largest group of people she had ever seen.

She recognized a few faces, but most of the crew members were strangers to her. A man in uniform approached.

"Zhiyu 1116, pilot engineer." He bowed.

"Alicia 4572, historical communications." Alicia also bowed.

Zhiyu motioned Alicia over to the nearest unused computer and pulled up the ship's telemetry readings.

"Here's our expected trajectory and here's our new trajectory."

Alicia could see that the new line was breaking towards the sun of the solar system. Zhiyu opened a different page.

"What we are seeing is higher than expected magnetic readings from the star. This is unlike anything we've ever experienced."

"Can we compensate? What do the Bechtel Protocol numbers say?"

Zhiyu was frustrated.

"The measurements are outside of the Protocol's limits. The numbers coming out are garbage. We will be flying blind without the Protocol."

"Zhiyu, I have a general understanding of the Bechtel Protocol, but I'm not a mathematician. I have no idea how to change its limits."

"I understand that you have contact with the one person who might change the limits, though. You are in contact with Sarah Bechtel?"

"Yes, but only in dream state. We are not allowed conscious contact. It is the bedrock rule of historical communication. The possibility of breaking our timeline is large."

"I understand. We are desperate."

Sarah was on the starship bridge in her dream. Many people were moving around. It felt different from her usual Alicia dreams, not as tied into Alicia's thoughts and more herself.

"Sarah?"

Never had Alicia spoken to her!

"Alicia?"

"Hi, Sarah. I know this seems strange, but I need to communicate directly with you. We are having a problem with your Protocol."

Sarah was stunned.

"Alicia, you've always been better at math than me. The Protocol comes from your knowledge."

Alicia laughed.

"You're wrong there! I can barely understand it. I gave you some kernels, but you grew this. You are the greatest mathematician in history, hands down. Our best mathematicians, hundreds of years later, only have a general understanding of it, but here we are, light years from home based on your math. We are in a difficult position right now. Look with me at this screen. On it are the composition numbers of the nearest star."

Sarah looked at the screen through Alicia's eyes.

"Why are the metals' composition numbers so high?"

"We don't know. The working theory is that the star subsumed high-metal planets or asteroids."

"Hmm. Even with that, the magnetic readings seem too high. I can see that they would be way beyond Protocol limits."

"That's exactly right, Sarah! Do you think you could correct the limits?"

Sarah thought about it for a few moments.

"Maybe. It will take some time, though."

"You take all the time you need, Sarah. Your timeline doesn't affect mine."

Sarah spent the next morning clearing her schedule of commitments.

She had spent the last twenty years defending the Bechtel Protocol and teaching a new generation of physics and math students. Most mathematicians accepted her system now.

Harder to leave behind were her positions on several boards focused on convincing governments and corporations of the necessity of large-scale changes to reverse the planet's accelerating climate change. What she hadn't realized until today was that she had become bored as a professor and pessimistic about humanity changing its course.

Alicia's problem was exciting and demanded her engagement. Sarah had a feeling that the starship was not enroute to "boldly go where no man has gone before," but the last vestige of human life. It was her obligation to save that humanity.

First, she would need to understand the magnetic anomaly…

"Alicia?"

"Hi, Sarah!"

"Sorry, that took a few more years than I thought. Here's what you need to do…"

In her dream, Sarah was Alicia standing on a hilltop. In the valley below was a small town, mostly domed buildings, but new construction with lumber framing was emerging on the outskirts. There were trees and grasses, slightly different from what she knew, but easily recognizable. The sun was high in the sky, larger than her own and tinted pink. A few clouds scuttled by.

ABOUT THE AUTHOR

James Zul is a writer and journalist who has balanced a rational and pragmatic work life with exposure to the abundant esoteric facets once common among ancient peoples.

"Sarah, we will never be able to thank you enough for what you've done for us. I feel I need to give you an explanation."

"That's not necessary, Alicia. I've been able to fill in the blanks over the years and lived long enough to see what is in store for us here. I've read some interesting articles on the possibility of telepathic connection to the minds of the deceased."

"We call it historical communication now."

"I am so happy for you, Alicia. All of you."

Both women were quiet for a few minutes, two minds in one body. The clouds got larger.

"Sarah, do you see any faces in the clouds?"

Scott Colley (he/him) has spent most of his life working in forestry and construction. Though a lifetime writer, he developed his love of writing while living alone and off-grid in Alaska for years. His interests outside of writing include travel, woodworking, and making a better world than the one we occupy now. He has lived in Oregon for twenty-five years.

Acknowledgements

This anthology wouldn't be possible without the support of the Emmons-Calandrino Family Trust. We're deeply grateful to be able to keep Cai's memory alive while giving other writers opportunities. Thank you.

Thanks also to the fab folks at Chill Subs for having us in their awesome contest club and offering free memberships to all entrants, as well as our contest winners.

Thank you to our band of volunteer judges, themselves writers and story-lovers, who carefully read and scored all the submissions. And to Miriam Gershow, our amazing final judge!

We're also deeply grateful to all the writers who entered the contest, who trusted us with their words.

Wordcrafters is committed to helping writers of all ages and levels tell the stories we each hold inside. Check out what we're up to at wordcrafters.org.